ISBN: 978-0-9955093-4-4
RANI GOES TO THE MELA (Book 1 of the Rani series)

Written by Shahida Rahman
www.shahidarahman.co.uk

Illustrations and cover design by Tanya Maneki

Edited by Ann Harth

Typesetting by Dave Hewer Design

Printed by Lightning Source UK

Published by **Safia Imprint**
An imprint of **Perfect Publishers**

23 Maitland Avenue
Cambridge
CB4 1TA
England

www.perfectpublishers.co.uk

Rani Goes to the Mela

By Shahida Rahman
Illustrated by Tanya Maneki
Edited by Ann Harth

"Would you like to be part of the mela, Rani?" her Mummy asked. "A mela is a kind of fair. You could walk in the parade or dance on the stage."

"Grandad says I'm too little," said Rani.

"What do you think, Rani?" asked Mummy.

"I am not little," thought Rani.

Music floated through the air and Rani sniffed the spicy smell of Indian food. She was hungry.

Her hand crept into her pocket and she jingled her money.

Just next to their stall was a fruit vendor.

Rani skipped over and looked. She loved the bright round oranges, the blushing mangoes, and the ripe yellow bananas.

Rani thought about buying a shiny red apple when she noticed a butterfly on one of the apples. It fluttered into the air and danced down the street. Rani laughed and ran after it.

sweet heaven

asmalai

fig halwa

nutty halwa

Rani followed the butterfly past stalls with crispy golden pakoras, chicken and lamb kebabs, and fried onion bhajis.

The stalls selling sweets came next: Rani saw creamy rasmalai, white balls of lemony rasgulla, and her favourite — sweet nutty halwa.

Rani tried to catch the butterfly, but it flew up and away. She gazed at the colours and the shiny jewels in a stall filled with beautiful bags and jewellery.

"I would love a bag like that," she said.

Rani's tummy rumbled. She walked to a samosa stall. Rani put her hand in her pocket and pulled out a shiny new coin. She handed it to the lady who gave her a warm samosa.

Rani ate the samosa, then looked around. Where was Mummy and Grandad's stall?

Silky saris and sparkling lenghas swept past, but she couldn't see Mummy and Grandad anywhere.

Rani started to cry.

A girl walked by carrying the most beautiful green and red bag Rani had ever seen.

"Are you lost?" the girl asked, seeing Rani's tears. Rani nodded. "Don't worry, little one," said the girl. "I'll help you find your mummy."

"My name is Annika," said the girl, as they searched for Mummy and Grandad.

"I'm Rani. I love your bag."

They saw jewellery, clothing and food, but they didn't see Mummy and Grandad.

"If you were in the parade, your family would find you," Annika said.

"I'm too little," said Rani.

"Then we will make you big."

"Here we are, at the stall!" said Annika.

"My little sister and I planned to be in the parade, but she couldn't come. She's not well. You can wear her costume."

Rani felt pretty in the lovely salwar kameez. "Thank you, Annika. I hope Mummy will see me."

"But how will I be big?" she wondered.

"Do you think you can walk on
stilts?"

Rani laughed. "I can try!"

Rani took a little step. "I can do it!" she said, walking in small circles.

"Now I'll be able to see Mummy and Grandad!"

"Let's go!" Annika said. "The parade's starting!"

"And I'm part of it!" said Rani.

"Wait," said Annika. "You need one more thing." She took off her bag and put it on Rani's neck. "Perfect!"

"Rani!" Mummy called. "I see you!"

Rani laughed. "I'm not too little, Mummy! I'm in the parade!"

The music played. Everyone danced and cheered.